TOWER OF GOLD AND GOBLINS

THE WINTER COURT SERIES, A COMPANION NOVELLA

CROWNS OF MAGIC UNIVERSE

ASHLEY MCLEO

MERAKI PRESS

Editing by Owl Eye Edits

Cover art by Sanja Gombar

Chapter art by Anna Spies of Altra Luna Art

Map by Cartographybird Maps

Ebook ISBN: 978-1-966080-13-8

Paperback ISBN: 978-1-966080-14-5

AUTHOR'S NOTE

This story is part of The Winter Court Series. It takes place during the events of book 3, A Hallow of Storm and Ruin, but did not fit structurally into that book.

This tale is from Lady Marit Armenil's point of view. It is about an unwanted forced marriage among fae nobles, breaking free from those chains, and finding a flame of romance on the other side. There is mention of non-consensual sex but it is not described.

<u>The Winter Court (Crowns of Magic Universe)</u>
A Kingdom of Frost and Malice
A Lord of Snow and Greed
A Hallow of Storm and Ruin
A Tower of Gold and Goblins - companion novella
A Crown of Ice and Fury

THE NORTH SEA
THE SNOWSWEPT LANDS OF
WINTER'S REALM
MAPPED IN THE PRESENT AGE
TO THE VAMPIRE KINGDOM
WESTERNLANDS
TRALISKA
HOUSE QIREN
GULDTOWN
HOUSE LISIKA
MIDLAN
GERSEMI
MINE
ODELIA
HOUSE
VAGLE
RIIS TOWER
REDMIST
MOUNTAINS
SISAVAL
LIEKOS
VITVIK
MYRR
HOUSE
BALIK
LOST KINGDOM
OF DERGIA

MAJOR SETTLEMENTS
MINOR SETTLEMENTS
NOTABLE LOCATIONS
MORIAL
HOUSE ARMENIL
VIRTORIS ISLAND
ORTHLANDS
LEIRE
HOUSE VIRTORIS
FARVERG
THE SHIVERING SEA
AVALDENN
THOR
LBORG
E AABERG'S
TRAL SEAT
BITRA
HOUSE RIIS
EASTERNLANDS
VANTALIA
STORMY BAY
UTHLANDS
GRINDAVIK
HOUSE ITHAMAI
ICE TOOTH
MOUNTAIN RANGE

CHAPTER 1

Would today be the day my husband killed me?

I stared out the window of my tower room, fingers trembling as they wove my long red tresses into their familiar braid. Just trying to summon the courage to go downstairs and breakfast with my lord husband felt like one frost giant sized task.

If only I could fly home.

But that was ridiculous. A faerie's wings were delicate, and mine wouldn't last an hour in the cold that had settled over the midlands of Winter's Realm. After my wings failed me, I'd be forced to run north for days, on foot, through the wilderness and frigid cold.

What really stopped me, however, was that if I ran, my entire family would be in danger. Likely killed. Victims of the King of Winter's icy wrath.

So, I settled for avoiding my husband as much as

possible. It was not proving too difficult. Upon his request, I broke my fast with him each morning, but so far, my husband had called me to that nauseating marriage bed only twice. Other nights, he sought the warmth of a mistress, whom he did not bother hiding from my sight.

Nothing turned out as I hoped. I swallowed, a sadness welling inside me.

I'd always prayed that I would marry a male who was handsome and gentle and sweet, but also strong, especially for those who needed his strength. One who loved me as much as the younglings I might bear. Younglings I'd always wanted, but now found myself wishing never came. Not if House Triam's blood flowed in their veins.

Handsome as he was, Lord Egil Triam was cruel and rumored to have killed three previous wives. I, for one, believed the whispers that swirled around my husband. He'd already shown himself to be dismissive and cold-hearted and selfish towards me. I hated every bone in my husband's body. Hated that the King of Winter's Realm had forced me to wed Jarl Triam, and I could do nothing about it.

Only one thing gave me peace: the fist-sized bag of mixed herbs hidden within the drawer of my spindle-legged desk. I had only needed to take the herbs twice, but I could still taste their bitter tang. An unpleasant lingering, though one that I'd endure gladly.

"Qildor," I spoke the name of the knight who had

passed me the herbs like a prayer as I finished my braid and tied up the end.

The noble knight had grown up being good friends with my brother Connan, and some of that affection had rubbed off on me when we were teenagers.

Back then, Qildor hadn't been a powerful knight, and I hadn't been a noble lady on the marriage mart. We'd simply been two younglings falling for one another.

I'd been so happy the night he'd given me my first kiss beneath a purple and green painted night sky. The feeling of his long black hair sliding between my fingers, his juniper scent, and his careful, loving touch would always be something I cherished, even if much had changed.

Now lovely, violet-eyed Qildor was a knight sworn to none other than the royal House of Aaberg. An elite Clawsguard. Respected and loved by so many for what he stood for.

And yet, his achievements did not save him from his own punishment. My blood ran cold at the memory of blood spraying on the throne room floor as the King of Winter whipped Sir Qildor for a transgression I'd also been guilty of.

A knock came at the door, making me stiffen and grasp the windowsill tightly. Slowly, I turned to face my tower suite, decorated heavily in a garish gold hue. Overcompensating in a way that was distasteful to my sensibilities.

"Lady Marit?" a voice came through the wood. "'Tis time to break your fast."

"I'd rather starve," I whispered, even as I patted down my plain black dress with long sleeves and a slightly flared skirt. To the Triam's, I was honoring one of their colors. To me, this was a mourning dress for my father.

By the dead gods, who would have guessed I'd miss the bland gray and white of my house? I pictured my old wardrobe, the light gray and dove white dresses adorned with running direwolves. Most of my clothes were in my childhood bedroom, a haven that also dripped with direwolf imagery. What I wouldn't give to wear them again. To see Father wearing our wolves. To be far from here, in the peaceful city of Morial, with my family.

"My lady?" the voice came again.

"Coming." I crossed the circular room, brushing my hand against the top of my golden velvet armchair as I went.

A goblin awaited me outside my door. A curiosity, indeed.

Most fae, especially nobles, thought of goblins as dirty and did not allow them near their homes. Where I'd grown up, we'd never employed a single goblin servant, and the only members of the goblin race that we'd entertained had been leprechauns—the sole sub-race of goblinkind that was accepted widely into society.

My husband, however, employed a great many

goblin servants, all with green skin, and a sharply pointed nose, ears, and teeth. This female had long white hair too.

And always wearing that chunky golden bangle. I stared down at her. *They all have the same one. I wonder if it's from their tribe?*

The goblin looked up, catching me staring at her, and making me blush.

"Uh, hi." I cast about for some reason that I might be watching her so closely. One that didn't display my ignorance to her kind. I landed on a question that was as natural as could be—one I was ashamed I hadn't asked earlier, in fact. "I realized that I don't know your name. I'm Marit."

"I'm Ardal, Lady Triam." The goblin curtsied and the corners of her green eyes crinkled at the corners.

"Lady Armenil," I corrected, and thanked the stars for the laws of the kingdom.

House Armenil was part of the Sacred Eight, and when members of the Sacred Eight married, they changed their family name only if they married someone with stronger magic than their own. I possessed weak winter magic, which ruled me out as the heir to House Armenil, but I *did* have strong earth magic. And more importantly, stronger magic than my husband.

Hence, I kept my last name. Of course, many outside the Sacred Eight would not realize or assume this, but I would be diligent in correcting them. Perhaps if I loved Egil Triam, things would have been different, but they were not.

"Apologies, my lady," Ardal replied. "Your class has strange ways that I know nothing of."

"I suppose you're right, but it's tradition." I replied. "You've shown me to breakfast and dinner more often than other goblins. Are you to be my personal maid?"

No one had introduced themselves as such. Or at all, come to think of it. Not that I had cared until today. Sorrow had clouded my thoughts, my sleep, my very being.

"I am, my lady. The jarl took a few days to decide who to assign permanently."

Days? Try weeks. Not that it was a surprise. I was not a priority for my husband, and he made sure I knew it.

We were rapidly approaching the breakfast room, and voices that did not belong to my husband or his pitchy mistress caught my ears.

"Who will I be dining with?" I asked Ardal.

"Lady Triam and my lord's sister arrived back from Odelia late last night," Ardal said. "They're breaking their fast with my lord."

CHAPTER 2

"*Finally*, she arrives," drawled the elder faerie at the table.

The female I assumed to be Lady Triam did not rise when I entered the room, all black and gold and as garishly decorated as my suite. Rather, she flicked her bony hand at the chair next to my husband.

I pressed my lips together. As I was now the lady of the house, Lady Idun was in my spot, at the head of the six-person table. Her direction stank of a power move that I did to appreciate, but I also didn't want to spoil any chance I'd have at a civil relationship within the household. I already despised her son, but maybe the mother wouldn't be so bad? Maybe she sat there out of habit? After all, it had likely been her place since she'd married.

I could let the slight slide this one time.

"My lord husband." I forced myself to take my seat

with the grace my mother had instilled in me. He did not look up from the parchment he'd been reading. "Introductions are in order, it seems?"

Lord Triam heaved an annoyed sigh and set down the paper. "Wife, this is my mother, Lady Idun Triam, and my younger sister, Gorina Triam."

"Lady Marit Armenil." I forced a smile.

Lady Idun, like her son and daughter, had a classically beautiful face. All of the Triam's boasted deep brown eyes and dark hair that shone in the light, though Egil's wings gleamed a brilliant sapphire blue while his mother's and sister's were pink.

"I hope your excursion into Odelia proved pleasurable?" I added as a goblin set toast and a bowl of fruit in front of me.

Lady Idun sneered and slapped at a goblin's hand as he tried to serve her tea. The hot liquid spilled on the goblin's arm, and he yelped, but Lady Idun paid him no mind. "You're a Triam now, Lady Marit."

"She's part of the Sacred Eight, Mother." Egil raised his eyebrows. "They do things differently." His tone was not defending me, but rather of slight resignation. Keeping my last name was a matter I'd fought him on and won.

"Bah! She should go by *our* name. Or is she too proud?" Her gaze narrowed upon me.

I was about to retort that I had no plans to take their name when Lady Gorina raised a limp hand.

My sister-in-law was quite small, her light pink wings a wreck. One was half missing and the other curled in on itself violently. Though I knew little of Gorina, I knew she was twenty-five turns of age, just like me. From her age and appearance, I deduced that she, like many around our age, was a victim of the blight. Perhaps that was why I hadn't seen her at the Courting Festival? She was like my younger brother Connan, too ill to attend?

Then again, she spent a week shopping. Doesn't seem too ill to me.

"When will her dowry arrive in our vault?" my new sister asked, and my bit of toast turned to sand in my mouth as my hopes that I'd be friends with *someone* in my new family vanished.

"I'm not sure," my husband replied as though I wasn't sitting right next to him. "Wife?"

I cleared my throat, the image of my father's head laying in a box resurfacing with vengeance. I tried not to think of his recent death, for it was too upsetting, and I was already fighting to remain myself in this new place, with my new, horrible husband and a life I did not love. "You may not know that my father was recently murdered, and my mother is now grieving the loss of her mate, so—"

Gorina rolled her eyes as she plucked a strip of bacon from her plate and twirled it around. "It's only a matter of visiting a coinary, is it not? Can't your mother send the heir to do it?"

"My brother was too ill to attend the Courting Festival." The words came out tighter than those before. "And now he's also grieving for our father, so I expect my dowry isn't the first thing on his mind."

"Send your family a raven demanding it," Lady Idun said. "Gorina and I spent heartily in Odelia. Our vault needs refilling."

"Do it today," my husband added. "And you will write to me when the dowry arrives."

I blinked. "Write to you? Will you not be here?"

He tossed down the parchment he'd been reading.

I picked it up, scanned the letter. The king had already asked my husband to collect taxes from the fae he governed in the midlands. Jarl Triam had done so, and since he'd returned to his home, had been collecting additional taxes within the city.

The king was now requesting the funds—as well as whatever fighting forces Jarl Triam gathered.

To fight an uprising. House Falk loyalists.

I took in those named as traitors to the realm. My friends' names.

"Is this real?" I asked.

"Of course it is," Jarl Triam replied. "I'm to go fight for the rightful ruler. And as requested, I will be taking nearly every fae in Liekos who can fight."

His mother, who had since begun eating her eggs, looked up. "What of our guard? If those dirty rebels attack I will not be left defenseless."

"A skeleton guard will remain, Mother. And if there's a true rebel fight the combined armies of King Magnus will descend and squash them!" His face shone with pride for a king that I hated. "To add to his efforts, any other male and female above the age of twenty will join me. The king has given me a highborn wife. I need to serve him loyally."

Stars, a war . . .

"Egil, our best earth fae are all male of fighting age. What will we do with the greenhouses?" my husband's mother prodded further.

A valid question. If one wanted fresh fruits and vegetables, greenhouses were essential in Winter's Realm. Each city had hundreds, and villages and towns always had enough to support their populations.

"My wife has earth magic. She will run them."

I gaped. "Liekos is a medium-sized city. I cannot run *them all*."

"Of course not. Underaged or old fae will help. But you will do your fair share. At the very least, you're in charge of the greenhouses for our home."

The Triams lived in a relatively small castle, but to feed all those who worked within, they still required ten greenhouses.

"That's too much."

"Are you already with youngling?" my mother-in-law asked, making my cheeks burn.

"I don't think so." I chose my words carefully for fae could not lie.

The herbs weren't one hundred percent effective, and the irregular cycles of fae females was a tricky matter, leaving me wiggle room for doubt. My cycle had not come for three months and very well may not arrive for another three. Only the dead gods knew. Until my bleeding arrived, or until I felt a life growing within me, I couldn't be sure if I was with child.

But by the dead gods, I hope not.

Lady Idun scowled. "Then you will do your share, and if my son says that's feeding fae in the castle, that's what you'll do."

I wanted to argue, but a better idea occurred. "If you're going to Frostveil Castle, perhaps I should come? Before I left to come here, Princess Saga mentioned that her mother, the queen, might require a new hand-maiden. Wouldn't that bring glory to House Triam?"

My husband barked out a laugh, making me jump before composing myself once more.

"Why do you laugh?"

"The princess might have said many things, wife, but as she's gone missing from Avaldenn, her words hold no weight."

My hand tightened around my fork. Saga was missing?

"Where did she go?"

"No one can say," the jarl shrugged. "And according to the latest news, I'd say that she's not that important to find. Not when some great houses are abandoning our king and fleeing for their castles."

The way his eyes locked on mine made rocks settle in my stomach. Was House Armenil one of those great houses? Weeks ago, we'd lost my father—the head of our house—and the king insulted my house by marrying me to Jarl Triam. Between those events, we had reason enough. And yet, I was surprised that my mother had possessed the wherewithal to travel to our home. She'd been in shambles when I left the capital.

"Who has abandoned our dear sweet king, my son?"

Dear and sweet, my arse.

"House Balik, House Virtoris, certain members of House Riis, and . . . my wife's kin." He shook his head as though he were truly saddened. "Another reason I cannot let you go to Avaldenn, Marit. What if your family learns you're there and they find a way to abduct you? We'd be torn apart before we got to know one another properly."

A humorless laugh climbed my throat, but I swallowed it. If I had my way, we'd cease knowing one another this instant. In fact, learning that so many members of the Sacred Eight great houses were abandoning the king did not worry me. Rather, it sparked hope.

Hope and ideas.

I no longer had to worry that the king might so easily strike against my family. If they'd left the capital, they would have gone north to Morial. Once there, the king could not punish anyone I loved. Not without sending armed forces anyway, and he would likely prefer to use those against the rebels.

My heart skipped a beat. Knowing my family was safe changed everything.

CHAPTER 3

I sent off a raven clutching the stars-damned letter requesting my dowry in its talons. As much as I despised complying, to deny the Triams would do nothing for me. However, I'd make certain that my dowry would be the last wealth the family would squeeze out of me.

My deplorable business done, I returned to my suite and began thinking about exactly *how* I'd escape my situation, only to be interrupted when Gorina barged into my room.

"We require your presence," my sister-in-law trilled and spun on her heels, taking in my room. "I must say, these accommodations are nicer than those of his other wives'. Lush, if it is a touch small."

My throat tightened. I tried not to think of my husband's previous three wives. Or how they had all died mysteriously.

"Why do you need me?"

Gorina twisted to face me, her expression reading almost as though she was surprised to find me there. In my own room. Where she'd sought *me* out.

Skies, the Triams were a strange bunch. Dangerous and strange, and I wanted to be far away from the lot.

"Mother and I are going shopping for dresses to wear to a gathering. Brother says that you must come."

"Why?" I had plenty of dresses, and while most were gray or white, there were a few that were not the colors of the House of the Direwolf. I did not need new ones.

"Appearances. Come now. Mother is waiting."

I shook my head, but followed Gorina from my room to find a trio of goblins waiting outside my door. My maid, whom I'd given a few hours off, was not one of them, though the others looked very similar to Ardal and wore the same golden bangle. I nodded to them, and two goblins, a female and a male, exchanged shocked glances. The other female blinked and looked away.

Lady Idun Triam was indeed waiting for us at the front of the castle, a now-familiar sneer on her face. "Come now. I wish for this to be done quickly."

I wondered why they needed dresses at all if they'd just returned from Odelia, a large city with some of the best seamstresses in the midlands, but said nothing. I had already deduced that challenging them in small ways would not be worth it. Not when I intended to flee soon. Plus, now that I considered it, being outside the castle could help me.

I'd been too distraught to take note of the streets in Liekos when I arrived. I could begin mapping the city out today.

We exited the castle, mother and daughter walking arm-in-arm in front of me, and as we passed through the gates, many stared. Mostly at me.

Since my arrival, I had not ventured into the city. Surely, some wondered what the new Lady of Liekos was up to. Or maybe if I was still alive.

The city itself was quite nice. Not as flashy as Avaldenn, which despite my situation I found welcoming. In many ways, this new place reminded me of home. A bit more rustic, if a city could be such a thing. Cozy. It lacked Morial's proximity to the ocean and the winds that came with such a position on the coast, but otherwise, the longhouses, the shops, the forges, and the stalls selling hand pies looked the same.

I was admiring a shop window when a figure appeared down a side street, allowing me a glimpse of a familiar profile, long black hair, and strong build.

Qildor? My lips parted in shock.

"By the dead gods, Trulo!" Lady Idun shrieked, ripping my attention to her in time to see her kick a goblin that had strayed too close so as not to be run over by a horse. "Keep away!"

The male goblin apologized, grabbing his side as he did so.

Torn but desperate, I peered down the side street again, only to find that the person I'd thought was Qildor was gone. Disappeared down another street or into a shop.

Or I only imagined him. I was just thinking of him . . .

"You're worthless," Lady Idun growled, and again, I turned my attention to her, still walking down the street as though she owned the ice-covered cobbles.

This was the second time I'd seen her hit a servant. A trend, not a reaction. One that was cruel and unnecessary. "There's no need to be violent towards him."

"Don't speak to me like that," Lady Idun spat, not bothering to look at me as she spoke. "You're living under our roof, and we have not a copper claw to show for it. I'll not take disrespect from you."

My shoulders squared, and I came up beside her. "I'll remind you, Lady Idun, that I am no commonborn fae you can boss around. I'm Marit Armenil, now the Lady of Liekos, and I demand that you treat *my servants* with respect."

For the first time, my mother-in-law smiled. *Smiled.* But not with her eyes, and certainly not with her heart. Her smile was as sharp as the sea serpent bone-handled dagger my dear friend Sayyida had taught me to use when the king first declared me betrothed to Jarl Triam.

Stars, I missed Sayyida, Saga, Neve, and the Balik sisters as much as my family.

"We're here!" Gorina sang, as if the altercation

between her mother and me were not occurring. Maybe she had not noticed. Gorina struck me as just as air headed as her mother was mean.

One of the female goblins rushed to open the doors for us. As we glided into the dress shop, I smiled down at her.

"Thank you," the goblin whispered.

I entered the shop, which smelled of a spicy perfume that brought to mind a childhood visit to sand-soaked dunes of the Summer Court.

"Lady Triam." The shopkeeper appeared from the back. The brownie was tall for her kind and impeccably dressed. "Wonderful to see you in! And you've brought Gorina and . . ."

"My son's wife, Lady Marit."

"Ah! The new Lady of Liekos!" The shopkeeper beamed, though I was sure she'd also gone a shade paler.

"We require dresses," Gorina said. "Ones we can wear for a gathering we're having. Also dresses we can wear to Avaldenn once the king crushes the rebellion."

"Six dresses then," the shopkeeper said. "What colors?"

"*Four*," Lady Idun corrected. "Gorina and I will be measured. Lady Marit is only here to sign the purchase form. The money is to be taken from her account."

She meant for my family to pay for her dress! The nerve.

"Actually, it will not," I retorted, heat blazing

through me. "I assume my husband has an account here?"

"He does," the shopkeeper said with a loud swallow. "He—"

"Do as I say, Cecia," Lady Idun snapped. "And go fetch silks. The best ones you have."

The shopkeeper nodded hurriedly and ran off, clearly glad to be away from us. I spun to argue with Lady Idun when she raised her hand to strike me.

I'd never been hit. Not outside of the minimal sparring training I'd done. And I had not been prepared for it now. My eyes squeezed shut as I braced, waited, but instead of a blow, Lady Idun shrieked.

"The insolence!"

I opened my eyes to find Trulo standing in front of me, magic shimmering in his hands and spreading out. Sweat dripped down his face, and I understood. The goblin shielded me.

"*Leave.*" Lady Idun glowered down at her servant. "Leave, and I will not bring down the whip."

Whip!?

Trulo twisted, caught my eye, and I took a step back, out of Lady Idun's reach. The goblin darted to the side and ran out the door.

"I'll be leaving too," I announced. "You have no need for me here."

The other two protested, but I was already out the door, not about to give into what they wanted. Not when I had an escape to plan.

CHAPTER 4

The sun rose over the horizon, painting the sky in brilliant orange and pink hues that cut through the blue and indigo of the night. Despite the warm brilliance of the sunrise, the same cold hardness I'd seen the day before lingered in my husband's eyes.

Since our wedding day, when I'd wept in front of him as I took my vows, the jarl had been spiteful and odious. I could not wait for him to leave Liekos. And I would not cry if he never returned from the war.

Not that I'll be here.

Yes, I lived here by order of the king, and the White Bear of Winter's Realm was fearsome to cross, indeed. But the king was preparing for war. One that he would wage against my friend. He would not have time to think of me. What was one runaway wife to a war between the ancient houses of Winter's Realm?

Already, I knew my birth house did not support King Magnus, so I wouldn't either.

The pack that stays together endures.

It did not hurt to know that if the rebels won the war, the new queen would issue me a divorce. So I planned to escape, return to my family, and help the rebels.

"Goodbye wife," the jarl said flatly. "Send a raven if you discover you're with child."

He made what he wanted so plain. Not me or a life together. A child. One that bore winter magic, like so many in my line did. A youngling with powers to elevate his own line.

Not happening.

I inclined my head in answer. Seemingly docile.

His lips brushed mine, hard and uncaring and all for show. When he turned to his mother and sister, the jarl smiled warmly as he bade them goodbye. All the while, I waited, counted the seconds, and when Jarl Triam entered his sleigh and it rode away to meet the small army waiting outside the gates, on the outskirts of Liekos, I loosed a breath.

I turned, intent on returning to my room to continue planning—perhaps I could get a city map from my maid?—but a hand wrapped around my wrist.

"To work then," Lady Idun said, as though I should know what in all the nine kingdoms she was talking about.

"Excuse me?"

"You're starting in the greenhouses today, Marit. Did you not listen when my son said he was taking the majority of our earth fae to war?" She pursed her lips. "A war against a fae whose wedding you attended. Fates, the least you can do to slough off that poor reputation is to grow food for our city."

Heat rose in my cheeks. "I don't regret standing with my friends." She scowled, but I continued. "Especially not when the Faetia blessed that union."

"You'll still work in the greenhouses, no matter what you say." Lady Idun snapped her fingers, and two soldiers appeared. They were young, too young to fight a war, but apparently old enough to arm the castle if something bad were to happen. Strong enough to remain behind and defend what was Jarl Triam's. "Show Lady Marit to the greenhouses. She's working there until dinner."

I gaped. "That's an entire day! I can't work magic for that long!"

"Then you'd do well to pace yourself." Lady Idun spun and strode for the castle door. Gorina, who had been watching the exchange, trailed behind her mother.

Well, I'd not have that.

"I wish to return to my rooms." I sidestepped one of the soldiers, only for the other to stop me.

"Apologies, Lady Marit, but the jarl gave orders that in his absence his mother was in charge."

"I'm *his wife*." Detest the title though I did, I'd use it to get what I wanted.

The soldier shrugged and had the grace to look conflicted. "That's what he said. Now, to the greenhouses?"

"Fine," I huffed, seeing that this was getting me nowhere. Maybe I could turn this to my advantage and gather information about the city from greenhouse workers.

My escorts led me around the castle and down a path cutting through a snow-covered garden. The greenhouses rose in the distance, two-story structures each as long as a ballroom.

"How many earth fae remain?" I asked.

Those strong enough to be soldiers left with my husband, but surely that was only a small portion of the fae with earth magic. If there was one thing winterborn and bred fae knew, it was that keeping those with earth magic healthy and happy was imperative for the health of us all. The soil in the far north of Isila was often frozen, and the greenhouses provided much food. Trade supplemented the rest of our fresh food.

"Seventy-five earth fae usually work in shifts in the greenhouses. My lord took half."

"Half!"

"Yes, Lady Triam. Th—"

"*Armenil*," I corrected.

"There are fewer fire and light fae too."

All essential for greenhouses to run properly. Fire fae kept the temperatures level. Light fae provided sunlight during long winter days. Sometimes water fae assisted too, but not always. Many cities had sprouted by rivers or the sea, but for those landlocked settlements, snow was abundant. Fae with lesser magics, no magics at all, and few skills were often hired to collect snow and melt it for various uses.

I entered the first building made of glass and, despite the pleasant warmth and humidity, my shoulders slumped. The vegetation wasn't in terrible shape, but many plants drooped. I supposed it was to be expected with the weather of Winter's Realm on the decline as of late. No matter how many earth, light, and fire fae worked together to provide food, we were nothing compared to the magic of our kingdom as a whole.

And now we have thirty-something earth fae to grow food for the castle. Likely parts of the city too.

An older faerie approached. His body sagged as he bowed. "Lady Armenil, we heard you'd be arriving to help. We can't thank you enough."

I exhaled. That this male had gotten my name right endeared me to him, and he— and all the fae in here— needed help. And as much as I despised my new family, I'd not let the commonfae suffer for Jarl Triam's choices. The Armenils took care of their people, and for the time being these fae were mine.

"Where can I start?"

My arms trembled as I pushed a bit more magic into the sprout, hoping it was enough to keep the tiny vegetable alive for the night.

An entire day had passed in the greenhouses. Like the other earth fae, I'd stopped for lunch and to relieve myself, but that was about it. Though I'd often helped in the greenhouses of Morial, especially during harvesting periods, I'd never worked so hard, and it showed. Sweat shone on my brow, and my magic felt depleted.

And we haven't even made it through all the greenhouses.

Dread filled me. It would take days to bring health to all the vegetation that the castle relied on. I dared not think of the greenhouses in the city or on the outskirts. Were they having the same issue?

"Lady Marit, I'm to bring you back to your tower," said a soldier, not the same one who had shown me to the greenhouses, though this one was just as young. Just as skinny and green. Just as unreassuring in his presence and strength.

I understood that Jarl Triam had been ordered to see his army north, but I hated that I had to agree with Lady Idun on one point. Had he really needed to take *all* of the best soldiers? What if rebels of an orc tribe attacked the city?

I finished what I'd been doing and allowed myself to be led inside the castle, barely noticing other fae bowing or curtsying for me as we passed. Exhaustion had settled so deep in my bones, all I wished to do was eat dinner in the privacy of my suite, then bathe and sleep. I'd wake early tomorrow and plan my escape then, with a clear head and no interruptions.

When I reached my tower, I was happy to find plates of food already waiting. The scent of roasted meats and vegetables made my mouth water. How had my maid known I'd want dinner right away? Ardal was far more prescient than I'd imagined.

I had time only to wash my hands in my bathroom sink when my mother-in-law arrived. And she wasn't alone.

"What's this?" I asked, watching fae after fae carry in pots.

"I require roses. Golden ones. You'll be working on that tonight so that I may showcase them at the dinner we're holding for a group of influential merchants in a few days' time."

I squared my shoulders. It was one thing to work in a greenhouse to help feed those in the castle. I did that because I did not wish for others to starve. But *roses*? I resented being forced to create decor.

"I'm too tired, so I will not be doing that." I sat at the table set for me.

"Oh, but you will." Lady Idun waved the others out of the room.

"You forget, I'm the lady of this castle."

"And yet, I'm the one with the power. Given to me by my son until he returns."

The truth was, even if Jarl Triam had not given his

mother power over his estate and the city, others were far more likely to follow her than me. Most didn't know me.

"Be that as it may," I retorted, "you cannot expect me to grow you, of all things, *roses*, when I'm this exhausted. Not if you plan for me to work in the greenhouses again tomorrow."

My mother-in-law came closer, her lips curled with disdain. "Let me make this clear, Marit, you will do as I ask tonight. If you don't, innocents will suffer." She curled a finger, and a figure appeared in the door. Trulo—the goblin she'd kicked.

"I have many more goblins living in this castle. You showed empathy to them earlier. Will you pull that away? Let them suffer because you're lazy?"

The goblin's face shone with terror, and a pit formed in my stomach. Cruelty ran thick through the blood of House Triam.

"Why would you harm your own servants?"

She shrugged. "They'll still be able to work."

By the dead gods. Lady Idun, like most fae, had a disdain for goblins, but most fae wouldn't go out of their way to harm them. I got the feeling she might relish torturing a lesser fae.

"Fine. I'll grow your bleeding roses, but I must eat first."

"I'll send someone for the bushes in the morning. If they're not overflowing with roses, then Trulo will find himself missing a finger or two." She marched out of my room, taking the servants with her.

The door shut behind them, and I had just breathed a sigh of relief when a click resonated through my chambers. My spine straightened.

Had she . . .

I went to the door and turned the handle, only to find it locked. Not only was I expected to work well into the night, but I was trapped in my room until Lady Idun said otherwise.

CHAPTER 5

y fingers trembled as another golden rose bloomed, full and lush.

Lovely as the flower was, I wanted to crush the petals and hurl them to the floor. To take all the effects in my room, so many of them the same gold as the roses, and hurl them out the window. Instead I fell back in a chair and tipped my head to the ceiling.

For two full days I'd worked tirelessly, expending magic for hours upon hours, only to be forced into my room at night and commanded to do the same. While I did not entirely mind working in the greenhouses—feeding others was always a noble purpose—I *despised* the personal tasks Lady Idun foisted upon me.

Conflict riddled my heart in many ways. I didn't want to see goblin servants hurt, but soon, I'd have to make my move. I'd been asking questions while I worked in the greenhouses and learned the layout of the city. Which gate was easiest to slip through. Which streets were quietest. I had the advantage that many in Liekos didn't know me by sight. Escaping with as few witnesses as possible was imperative.

A soft knock came at the door, interrupting my planning. Each night since my husband left, his mother had locked me in my tower room and gave limited access only to my maid. Ardal arrived each night to draw me a bath and take my dirty plates.

"Yes?" I asked, not bothering to rise.

The lock turned, and the door opened. As I expected, Ardal appeared, though this time she held a box. "I thought my lady might need a bit more food. You've been working so hard."

Only then did I catch the scent of food. "Is that *cake*?"

"Chocolate," the goblin affirmed. "And more rolls. You might want to hide them." She nodded to the desk, her eyebrows raising.

My heart stopped. My bag of contraceptive herbs was in a desk drawer.

"Your secret is safe with me." Ardal took the plate of cake from the box and handed it over. A fork followed before I could ask. "I'd choose the same."

Embarrassingly quickly, tears formed. "Thank you."

I sat in my armchair, took a bite of the cake, and moaned. Delicious.

"I can draw a bath for my lady?" Ardal asked, pity plain in her tone.

"That would be nice, thank you." I pointed to the plate of cake. "I hope you don't get in trouble for bringing this. I wouldn't want Lady Idun to cut your pay or something."

Ardal smiled weakly. "I don't earn pay, my lady. But even if I did, I'd bring you a sweet. You earned it, and don't worry about me. I know my way around the castle well and was careful not to be seen with the cake." Her gaze strayed to the far wall, where there was nothing, before skirting back to me.

"Does she send the pay to your family?" I took another bite.

"No, my lady. You misunderstand. I'm not a paid servant, but a slave."

I choked on my cake.

In the Kingdom of Winter, slaves existed, but they were always human. *Not* a race of fae. It was against our laws to enslave one of our own magical order. And as for the humans, they were slaves because, as horrible as it was, no fae saw them as equals.

Most humans ended up in Isila by sheer chance, and once they'd eaten our food, they could not return to their own realm. While I'd never been to the human world, I'd been told it was nothing like ours. Isila was no place for beings with no magic or means of defense against the many monsters roaming our realm.

Ardal turned to fill the bath, taking my silence as . . . well, I wasn't sure what she thought of my silence.

"Wait," I said, stopping her. "I understand that

goblins don't usually live among other fae in cities, but it's still illegal to keep other fae races as slaves. How long have you been enslaved and how did this happen?"

"Long ago, the leader of our tribe made a bad deal with Jarl Triam. Since then, we have been paying for it." She lifted her arm, and the golden bracelet caught the candlelight. "Until these are removed, we are bound to House Triam."

"That's a mark of your enslavement," I gasped.

"A magical bind. As long as these are on our wrists, we cannot leave Liekos and must sleep in this castle each night, so even if one of us ran from the castle, it would only be temporary freedom."

"What happens if you aren't here at night?"

"We die."

My stomach hardened. "How many of your tribe are there?"

Ardal's face fell. "Now, only about fifty. There used to be four times as many."

Bleeding skies. I pushed the cake away.

"I'm so sorry." I now understood why the goblin Lady Idun threatened didn't simply leave his employment. He wasn't employed at all but forced to remain here. "I wish there was something I could do."

"It's not your apology to make," Ardal said, her face soft with sorrow. "We goblins can see you have a good heart, Lady Marit. That you're not like your new family."

"I wouldn't enslave you, if that's what you mean," I murmured. But as I spoke the words, they struck me as hypocritical. My family had human slaves. Not many, and we would never hurt them, but they were still living in our castle. Still *not free*. We called it protection from the harsh wilds of Isila and other fae who might take advantage of them—but was it, really?

"We know that."

"How can you be sure, though? None of you know me at all." Her kindness made me feel worse.

"You stood up for Trulo. Then you spend hours growing roses so Lady Triam does not hurt one of us. Small kindnesses go a long way with the goblins, and you're the first faerie in this family to be kind to any of us."

Now that the initial shock had passed, anger rose. I wasn't a slave, but I *was* being kept here against my will. And many females had died in this place. Why was the Triam family allowed to get away with mistreating others so?

"So, if you can remove the bracelets, you're free?"

"That's right."

"Is there a way you can take the bracelets off?" They didn't look too tight. Perhaps I could work my earth magic in a new way and bend the metal?

Ardal shook her head. "The only way the bracelets come off is if a member of the Triam family signs a document freeing us."

Well, I was a member of the family. Against my free will, but it still counted.

"Where's the document?"

"In the coinary." Ardal pointed a long finger at the window.

When I didn't speak again, Ardal wandered into the bathroom to run my bath. As the water poured from the faucet, I stood and went to the window. Darkness shrouded Liekos, but the top of the coinary with its white cauldron gleamed in the moonlight.

"Ardal?" I called, leaving the window and moving toward the bathroom.

"Yes, my lady?"

"If I ask you to remain quiet about a favor, will you?"

"I am your maid, my lady."

"Even if Lady Triam asks?"

Fear flickered across her face. Though it was unfair of me to ask for help, I needed it. Needed her. Ardal wasn't a friend. That was too close a designation for someone I'd only been speaking to for a few days, but she *was* the closest thing I had to one in this city.

"Please," I whispered.

"What is it?"

"I need a map of Liekos," I said. I'd been gathering knowledge, but it wasn't enough to make me feel certain. Especially not if I added an extra stop to my escape route. "A current one."

Her green eyes pierced me, seeing far too much for my liking. "You mean to run."

I swallowed. "I do."

Silence fell between us for what felt like an age. I didn't dare tell her that if the rough beginnings of my plan worked, she would be helped too. Because what if I failed? What if my name wasn't good enough? I brought her hopes up only to be unable to deliver?

Ardal sighed. "I can't fault you for doing what I wish I could do too. I'll help, but please, if the item is found before you leave don't mention me?"

"I would never."

She cocked her head and stayed silent for thirty long seconds before replying, "It's shocking, even to me, but I believe you."

CHAPTER 6

FIVE LONG DAYS LATER

My cloak, black, made of thick wool, swished around my ankles. One might have thought I chose the cloak because it was unremarkable, and I did not wish to get dirt on my finer ones while I worked in the greenhouses. That could not be further from the truth.

Since Ardal had given me a map of the city, I'd studied it nightly, and the day had come for me to make my move. To go to the coinary, free the goblins, and escape Liekos. To flee into the wilds of Winter's Realm.

Down to my undergarments, I was dressed warmly and inconspicuously, so as not to draw attention. Anything valuable from my family, I carried in the over-sized interior pockets of my cloak, or in the pockets of the trousers that I wore beneath my dress.

But no matter how much I wanted to distance myself from the Triam family, I planned to visit the greenhouses first. For my peace of mind, I needed to be certain that all the work I'd been putting into the vegetation had taken. After all, I did not wish for the commonfae to suffer, and there was no denying that I had made a difference. I hoped they could keep up the good work once I fled.

It will help if they have fifty fewer goblins to feed. I allowed a small smile to grace my lips as I entered the first greenhouse.

The humid air filled my lungs as I breathed in. In some ways, I'd miss coming here daily. The scents of fresh greenery, flowers, and ripening fruit were so alluring.

"Where will you be today, my lady?" The elder faerie who had welcomed me to the greenhouses the first day approached. He did not look quite as exhausted as before. Now that the plants were finally growing well, we needed to put less magic into them.

"At first glance, this greenhouse looks good," I answered after a brief scan. "I think I'll move to number six."

A tactical choice. Number six was right by the stables.

"I'll remain here then," the faerie said. "The lettuce needs more attention. Lady Idun requires much of it for her dinner tonight."

I refrained from rolling my eyes, but only just. Tonight was the merchant dinner I'd been growing heaps of roses for. If only I could wilt them before I ran.

I left the greenhouse, bracing against the cold that deepened by the day and routinely sucked the breath out of me. Little daggers penetrated my lungs as I breathed in again. I was already uncomfortable, and didn't like to think what that meant for my journey. Not that I was changing my plan. As I closed in on greenhouse number six, the stench of the stables grew. My nose wrinkled. I much preferred the scent of plants to animals.

Slipping into the greenhouse, I let loose a breath, savoring the smell of soil and the warmth while I still could. Soon, I'd be riding north on horseback for hours at a time. I had enough coin to buy shelter for the night on the way, but getting between cities and towns would be quite uncomfortable. Dangerous too. Besides the temperature, wild orc and goblin tribes ranged the midlands, as well as other nameless monsters.

It's this or staying here. Being mistreated and waiting for a husband I hate to return.

The choice, if one could call it that, was easy.

I worked my magic in greenhouse six for a bit, making sure that many saw me. As I went, I stuffed a couple of apples from the orchard section of the greenhouse into my oversized cloak pocket. I already had cheese and *levae* bread, both secreted to me by Ardal, but extra food never hurt. After two hours, I recognized I was no longer preparing, but stalling. That would not do.

The sooner I left the city, the farther away I got

before dinner. Once night fell and I failed to show up at my tower, Ardal would be forced to notify Lady Idun, and my mother-in-law would act.

I walked back towards the greenhouse door. A few workers saw me, but none appeared bothered or suspicious about my leaving. For the past four days, I'd made it a point to work between greenhouses. So when I slipped out of number six, I pulled my hood up and veered toward the stable without so much as a glance over my shoulder.

Although I put on quite a show of confidence, I was relieved that when I entered the massive stables, no one was around.

I stopped briefly before two gryphons. Racing stock, I was sure. Would that I could fly from Liekos, but unless one had elven blood or an elf to speak with the creatures on their behalf, gryphons were notoriously temperamental. As I was a pureblooded faerie with no elven ancestry, I did not try. Besides, I still had to stop at the coinary, and I could not show up there on a gryphon's back.

It took only minutes to find a horse that was about the size I was used to riding. Her saddle hung by her stall. I hoisted it off the hook and slowly approached the mare.

She remained docile as I slid the saddle over her. She was well trained, which allowed me to breathe easier. I just hoped she was fast too.

Minutes later, I was trotting from the stables, hood

up, bright red hair tucked down my back, eyes downcast.

Due to the worsening weather, the grounds were rather empty. *A blessing from the stars,* I thought, as I approached the gate.

As I'd been kept in the castle during most of my time in Liekos, I was not too worried that the fae at the gate would know me. Still, when the fae called for me to stop, I forced myself to remain loose. Not guilty. Outwardly calm, even if my heart was threatening to fling out of my chest.

"Where are you off to with mi' lord's horse?" one of the guards called, clearly bored, just doing what his job entailed.

"I'm to deliver a message for the Lady of Liekos," I said, not specifying which lady, planning my message to be one that the leprechauns of the coinary received from myself.

"Alright then," the guard drawled. "Go on."

I blinked. I'd been prepared to twist the truth as far as possible, but the guard seemed not to care. My lord husband's choice to leave behind a skeleton guard of second-rate soldiers would be his loss.

I rode through the gates and down the narrow street that funneled into the city. Even from ground level, one could see the top of the coinary gleaming above the other roofs. I made my way there, careful not to make eye contact with anyone. The only people I wanted knowing my identity were the leprechauns of the coinary.

Thankfully, the fae of Liekos appeared to be lost in their own worlds. Actually, many walked with no spring in their step and harsh lines on their faces. I wondered how many had sent away a soldier and were worried over their loved one?

I reached the coinary, dismounted from my mare, and tied her up. In front of any other establishment, I'd want someone to watch over my horse, but no one dared steal from a coinary, and that applied to outside the establishments too.

Stepping inside, I exhaled before striding down the long white hall to where I knew many leprechauns would be at their desks, waiting to help their wealthy clients.

"Hello, miss. How may I help you?" a leprechaun presented at the end of the hallway, as they always did. Miserly they may be, but the leprechauns knew how to keep their clients happy.

"I'm here to sign a document," I said quietly, hoping that before he asked me my name, he'd take me to his desk, which would be enchanted to keep conversations private. I needed to remain anonymous for as long as possible.

"You hold a vault?"

"I do," I replied, though it would not be my vault that I was accessing today.

"Very good. My name is Coinmaster Gultz. Come

with me." He led me to his desk, within the bubble of the enchantments. I sighed with relief. So far, so good.

"Your name, miss?" the leprechaun asked.

"Lady Marit Armenil," I replied, my tone stronger than before. "But I'm here on behalf of my husband's house. The Triam family."

The Coinmaster's eyes, a brown so dark they were almost black, widened. He made to stand—to bow, I was sure, because that was what my rank demanded, but I held up a hand.

"Please, I wish to remain inconspicuous."

"Apologies that I did not recognize you, Lady Armenil." Coinmaster Gultz swallowed.

"No need to apologize. May we proceed?"

"Of course. What's the document that you require?"

"I wish to see the document pertaining to the enslavement of the goblins at my husband's castle."

His thin lips parted. "The one that details their enslavement?"

I understood his shock. Leprechauns were, technically, a sub-race of goblins. They had carved out a place in society, but I suspected many lived in fear that they'd be ostracized like other goblins. That they may, if the tables turned, be like the goblin tribes living and dying in the wilds.

I leaned forward. "I wish to sign the document to free them. As I am Jarl Triam's wife, that's possible, correct?"

I hadn't been able to shake the thought that Jarl Triam would have foreseen this act and put a rule in place to stop me. After all, he *had* put his mother in charge of his estate, so clearly he didn't respect or trust me.

"You're wed. No matter what name you use, you are a part of Jarl Triam's house and noble. As such, you possess the power that comes with that status." The Coinmaster replied, a smile growing on his face as he gave the answer I'd been hoping to hear.

The leprechaun gestured to the cauldron on the edge of his desk, white as snow, like the one on the roof of each coinary across the kingdom. He then pulled a small blade from his desk drawer. "You must prove your identity."

I placed a hand on the cauldron and knew the moment the cauldron had confirmed my identity because Coinmaster Gultz hopped off his chair and bowed.

"I shall return, Lady Armenil."

"Thank you."

He strode for The Below, as the area where the vaults were located was called. I was glad that I didn't have to join him. Monsters and foul magic often guarded The Below, and I did not like being down there.

The minutes passed, and my skin crawled. I didn't think the leprechaun would work against me, but there was a very small chance that Lady Triam or her daughter might enter the coinary. The urge to pull my hood tighter around my face overwhelmed me, but that would look too suspicious, so I sat there and waited, my blood pounding in my ears. When Coinmaster Gultz reappeared my muscles loosened.

He joined me and rolled out a scroll of parchment flat on the desk. "My lady, I do not mean to presume that you haven't considered the ramifications of your actions, but I must say something."

"Go on."

"The moment you sign this, the bracelets those goblins wear will fall from their wrists. They'll flee, and —if you had not considered doing so before—you should too." His gaze locked with mine, his expression dire. "Brides do not do well in the House of Triam. I'd assume especially not those who cause their new family troubles."

"We're of the same mind, Coinmaster. Do you have a quill?"

He handed me one from a phoenix. "Sign there and there and the enslavement will be void."

Wondering what Ardal's face would look like when her bracelet fell off, I signed with a flourish. Once done, I set the quill down, my heart thrumming.

Never had I felt like I'd done something so powerful. Had such a purpose. And as the ink on the document glowed gold, I smirked.

"It's done." The leprechaun patted the parchment

softly. "Now, my lady, I suggest that you waste no time and escape the city."

CHAPTER 7

I rode at a brisk trot through the streets.

Lady Idun may not yet know that I'd been the one to free her goblin slaves, but she'd soon learn. I knew from experience that my father, stars rest his soul, had eyes all around the city where we lived. Lady Idun was likely the same.

"Burning stars!" I called as a sleigh filled with adolescent males pulled out of an alley in front of me and I had to pull back hard on the reins. An overpowering stench of sour ale and sweat came off them in waves. I wrinkled my nose. "Watch where you're going."

One male, a handsome satyr, wagged his eyebrows at me and swayed as he stood to wave me over. "Maybe we'll go where you're going, beautiful. Care for company?"

By the dead gods, they hadn't just been drinking a

few ales. They were dead drunk. From the evening before, if their bedraggled states were any sign.

I scowled, and didn't deign to reply as I rode onwards.

"Miss, please!" Another voice called out just as I heard the satyr command the sleigh driver to follow me. "My friend's an idiot, but can you blame him? He— hey!"

"She's not interested," a familiar voice growled.

My heart leapt, and I twisted to find a familiar face emerging from the crowd of fae on the street. "Qildor!?"

I hadn't mistaken someone else for him. He was here!

The knight gave me half a grin before gesturing with his sword for the sleigh to turnabout. The young males were drunk, but not so stupid as to fight with a knight on horseback. The satyr, cheeks flaming, commanded the sleigh driver to move along. The driver did so happily, and they turned down another street, disappearing into the city.

"What are you doing here?" I whispered as the knight rode to meet me.

"The better question is, what are you doing right now, Marit?" His violet eyes, framed by unfairly long lashes, took in the surrounding area with care. "Because it looks like you're running away. Alone, at that."

"I am," I said. "And you're slowing me down."

"Bleeding skies," Qildor hissed, though amusement

tugged at his lips. "I came to get you to safety, but of course you'd do it alone. Please tell me that you have a plan?"

"I have a plan." I gestured for him to ride alongside me. "Did Connan send you?"

Before I'd journeyed to Liekos, one of my other brothers, Rune, had signaled that they'd come for me. I suspected that since my family had also fled Avaldenn, Rune had since spoken with Connan, the new Head of House Armenil. And Connan had gotten in touch with Qildor, his childhood friend and a skilled knight—

I gasped. "Qildor! You're *a Clawsguard*. You can't be here!"

He snorted. "As if I'd fight for a king who did this to you. Or one set on killing his son's own wife."

Only then did I notice he wasn't wearing his gold cloak or the elaborate pin that all Clawsguards wore. The pin was fashioned of pure gold and shape like a bear's claw to represent the royal House of Aaberg. "You—you've forsaken your vows to the royals?"

"I have." We turned down a side street, passing by a small cart from which a faun sold roasted chicken and turnips. "For the record, Connan didn't send me. Before your family fled Avaldenn, I told Rune I'd be the one to retrieve you. He agreed that was the best course of action. I'm sure Connan would have too, had he been at court."

"Oh." I breathed, my face flushing. The news was both flattering and horrifying. By forsaking the

Clawsguards, Qildor had not only tossed away his life's dream, but deserted. Broken an oath. If the king ever saw him again, Qildor would lose his head and be denied a Sigling ritual that would send him to the afterworld. "You risked too much for me."

He met my eyes, all seriousness and brilliant, shining steel. "While I may no longer live in Morial, your family is mine. I may not have been able to save you from abuse at that monster's hands, but I can take you to safety now."

A lump formed in my throat. All my life, family had surrounded me. My wolf pack. While we were not perfect, we were there for each other, and though another lady might hate their family for not fighting for them and allowing their forced marriage to go through, I did not.

House Armenil had been through too much for me to blame my grieving mother. It was my terrible luck that we'd lost my father, the very backbone of our family, shattering each of us in our own way, right when I'd been forced to wed. Mother had lost her mate and was in no condition to take on the king. Even if she had kept her wits about her, she had five other children's safety to consider.

In the weeks I'd been in Liekos, I'd felt so very alone. But with Qildor here, that weight lessened a touch.

"So what's the plan?" Qildor asked.

"The eastern gate is the weakest," I said on the back

of a breath that turned white in the cold winter air. To one side of the street, a merchant yelled about some sale he was having. "We're going in that direction now."

His eyebrows, dark and straight, pinched together. "If you were coming from the castle and heading east, you would not have been on the road I found you on. Right outside the door to my inn."

He'd been studying maps of the city too. "I made a stop at the coinary."

"You couldn't get coin from the castle, rather than give away your identity?"

"I didn't go for coin. I signed a contract to free slaves at the castle." I elaborated as we wove through the streets. When I was done, Qildor's face had gone hard.

"House Triam has a poor reputation, but I did not expect that they'd enslave other fae."

"No longer." My lips curled up self-satisfactorily.

"Thanks to you."

"Yes, well, it was the right thing to do." A small part of me feared I hadn't always chosen the right path. My choice felt like a small act of bravery, and a moment of discovering what I really thought. Still, I didn't want to make too much of it when I was ashamed of my past.

"I'm so glad to have you with me on the journey north," I admitted, and maneuvered my mare around a sleigh that was traveling slowly down the center of the street.

Qildor split from me, but when we came back together in front of the sleigh, he shook his head. His curtain of long, shiny black hair slithered against the fur of his cloak in a way that made me want to touch it. "We can't go north. We'd never make it."

"What? Why?"

"Armies are journeying to Avaldenn from all around the kingdom. There is too large a chance we'll come across one. Besides that, once Lady Idun knows you're gone, that's the way she'll expect you to go. She'll send a hunting party."

I chewed on my bottom lip. Of course, I'd considered the armies, but with so few guards and soldiers about would she really send out a hunting party?

"Where were you going to take me, then?" My stomach tightened as we turned the last corner, the eastern gate now in sight.

"South. To Myrr."

"To House Balik. How are they safe if they left the court in Avaldenn too?"

"It's a much greater distance between Myrr and Avaldenn. Not to mention their castle is impenetrable. They're your kin. You'll be safest there."

"I see," I said, unable to repress the sadness that welled up inside me. Although I counted some members of the Golden House as my best friends, and loved them, I'd truly wished to see my family. "I suppose—"

"Stop where you are!" An arrow shot into the ground, right in front of my mare. She reared, and my hood fell back, exposing my head and face as I held on to the reins for dear life, wrestling control back.

"The runaway bride!" a voice shrieked as my mare's hooves hit the ground hard, jostling me in both body and soul.

My heart leapt into my throat. *No! How did they find me so quickly?*

"Marit, this way!" Qildor's horse turned sharply, his face tight with fear. "We'll hide. We'll—"

"Go!" I backed up my mare. "Go before they see you with me. You cannot be captured, Qildor. She'll imprison you."

He'd deserted the Clawsguards. While Lady Idun did not know that yet, it would not be difficult to discover, and if she did . . . Qildor was a traitor to a brotherhood. She, as a lady of noble birth, would be within her rights to take his head.

"I can't leave you."

"*You will*," I gritted my teeth. If this gate had been on the lookout for me, the others would be too. I had no way out.

Knowing all that, my wings teased through my cloak, and I flew upwards, only to land on the ground and wait for the soldiers who were now running toward me.

"*Marit!*" Qildor tried once more.

"Go, before they see your face. I cannot bear to watch you die."

He looked like he was about to argue again, but the

soldiers were closing in. One raised his bow, and an arrow flew, just missing Qildor's head. His face turned white with rage.

"I'll find a way to free you."

"I know you will," I said, though I was not really sure. I only wanted him to leave. To be safe.

He kicked his horse in the sides, and they took off down the streets of Liekos as I stood in the street, waiting to be apprehended.

CHAPTER 8

"Y ou wench!" Lady Idun shrieked as two young soldiers brought me to a small room used for receiving guests. Near the door two servants watched, fear plain in their eyes. "How dare you try to leave Liekos!"

My chin lifted in defiance. "Why would I wish to stay? You work me day and night, like a slave."

"Leave us," the lady said to the others. "Stay outside the door."

"Our reward, Lady Idun?" One soldier asked confidently and stupidly.

She glared at them. "You will get your reward when I say you'll get it. *Now, leave.*"

Each fae filed out, a servant shutting the door behind them, until I was alone with my mother-in-law.

"You did this, didn't you?" Lady Idun growled. "You freed the goblins."

"Slaves you should never have had in the first place," I retorted.

"As if anyone cares about goblins."

"I do," I said, surprising myself. "Only humans can be slaves."

Though what I said was the law, and had been since before I was born, stating such a thing so plainly tasted bitter. Wrong. Coming to Liekos had opened my eyes.

Lady Idun marched closer, her heels clicking on the stone floor. Her face was crimson, and I half expected her to scream in my face.

What I did not expect was her hand to draw back and release. The slap stung, and though tears built in my eyes, I snarled.

"How dare you touch me like that!"

"You! You're nothing, girl. You're——"

"*I* am Marit Armenil." I growled, and my tone surprised me, it was so deep and furious. "Daughter of Lord Sten and Lady Orla of the Sacred Eight. You know as well as I do that the blood in my veins is valuable and exactly why I'm here. Your vile son wants Sacred Eight blood in his line."

"Your blood is the only valuable thing about you," my mother-in-law hissed. "But know this—the moment we get what we want from you is when we no longer have a use for that *precious blood*. Wouldn't it be a shame if some of it . . . spilled?"

I drew back, only for Lady Idun to snarl with unmasked pleasure.

"Guards!"

The door opened.

"Hold her down."

My wings teased through the slits in my thick cloak, but I was not fast enough. Before I flew out the door, the guards were upon me again, shoving me to the floor. My knees cracked on stone, and I yelped as hands gripped my shoulders.

Lady Idun eyed my wings. "I cannot harm you in some places. Those that may produce a child." She rounded the guards, and I sucked in a breath as her fingers gripped my right wing. "But you won't be needing your wings for that, will you?"

Pain stabbed through me as she pulled a dagger from one of the guard's sheaths and ripped through the tender flesh of my right wing. Tears fell down my face, and my breathing came fast and shallow. By the dead gods, this female was a monster.

A point she hammered home when she took my chin in her hand and with the other clawed my left cheek. A sob ripped up my throat.

"Put her in her room and lock the doors," Lady Idun commanded.

I didn't fight as the guards lifted me by my armpits and dragged me away.

I stared out the window, desperation raking over me.

Hours had passed since Lady Idun's assault. Hours since I'd been tossed into my tower and locked away.

Will I ever leave this tower? This castle?

Lady Triam had made it clear that after I birthed a youngling, or maybe a few younglings, their family would have no interest in keeping me around. No doubt I'd die like my husband's previous wives.

I swallowed as my wing throbbed again. I was stuck here. The only way out being the window and with only one working wing, and a four-story drop, I could not fly out. If I did, even if I survived the fall, I'd likely be in no condition to run.

Not to mention the guards.

Lady Idun had altered the guard's routes around the grounds. I'd seen three different guards walk by in as many hours. It made me wonder if someone had seen Qildor and told Lady Triam that I hadn't been alone.

A scraping of wood on stone made me jump and turn. The door remained shut.

"Over here," a voice I recognized whispered. "On the other side of the bed."

I pivoted and gasped as Ardal emerged from a hidden door that came up to my knees. Her wrist was free of her bracelet.

"What are you still doing here? You should've run!"

"I did," she admitted. "We all did. But then I heard you were taken and hurt, and I couldn't leave you. So I snuck back into the castle using one of the servants' entrances."

"Has that door always been there?" I asked.

The goblin approached; her lips turned down as she took in the four cuts on my cheek. "It has. Lord Triam prefers we use them when traveling the halls alone, though his mother does not. She doesn't like to be surprised. They're all over the castle, though. It was how I so often snuck treats by her."

I blinked. Yes, come to think of it, I had seen the goblins more once my husband left his castle.

"I have something to clean your wounds." Ardal slipped a beaten-up leather bag off her shoulder and opened it to reveal a bottle and clean towels. "May I?"

"Please," I sighed. "I wouldn't want them to get infected. But be careful with my wings?"

"Of course. Sit."

I did as she requested and the goblin began to gently, oh so gently, clean my wings. Beneath her touch, emotion welled inside me again.

She was free, Ardal and all the others, and while I pitied my situation, for them I felt only joy. Joy and shock that my maid had returned to see to my wellbeing.

"We're all thankful for what you did, Lady Marit," Ardal said after a few moments of silence. "The second the bracelet fell off, well, I almost couldn't believe it, but it was real. You freed us—to your own detriment."

"No," I whispered, agony rippling across my face. "Please don't think like that."

"You lost time going to the coinary."

"I lost time elsewhere too. I don't regret freeing you. In fact, it's the only good thing to come of this."

Ardal's soft touch on my wing paused, and she rounded the chair to face me. "You mean you lost time with that other faerie?"

My eyes widened. "How do you know about him?"

"When we ran from the castle, we had to seek refuge in homes in the city. We can't all flee into the forest at the same time, so we're slipping out as we can. The home I'm hiding in until I can make a break for it is by the eastern gate. They saw you before you were caught, talking to a male faerie."

"His name is Sir Qildor."

"A knight then?"

"Yes, he's a family friend. He——" I sucked in a breath, as an idea formed. "I know where he's staying, Ardal. Can you get a message to him?"

"You showed us kindness when no one else did. Even when you weren't sure why you were doing it." I swallowed, discomforted that she saw me so clearly. "I'll do anything for you, Lady Marit."

She thought too much of me, but that didn't mean I would not seize this chance. Meager though it was.

"Tell Sir Qildor where I'm being kept. He's cunning and strong, and, with enough time to work things out, may be able to free me."

Ardal nodded. "Tell me where to find your knight."

CHAPTER 9

Glass shattered, and I shot up from where I'd fallen asleep at my desk. Heart pounding, I pushed the chair back. Had Lady Idun arrived to punish me again? Or she'd sent an assassin to do away with me already?

"Marit!" a masculine voice cut through my panic.

"Qildor?" I squeaked.

In response, more glass shattered, creating a hole large enough for his head to poke through.

I sucked in a breath and, as he broke more glass to enter, I rushed to the window to meet him. "Ardal found you already?!"

"As I was having dinner."

So only a bell after I'd spoken with the maid. She worked quickly.

"The goblin told me the hour the castle guard changed." Qildor extended his hand. "I waited until the new gate guards took up their posts and knocked them out and left the gates ajar for an easy escape, but we must still move quickly. Others are still walking the grounds. If we take too long, they'll find them and raise an alarm."

I nodded, elated that this was happening and so soon. I'd hoped Qildor would come but expected it would take him days to plan. Maybe weeks.

"Out the window then?" I asked, the wind teasing inside.

"Horses are waiting below. It's too cold to fly further than a few blocks." He undid his weapon belt. "You know how to use them now, so you won't be going anywhere unarmed any longer."

He handed me the belt, on which were sheathed two daggers. My chest tightened. Qildor was right in that before I'd left Frostveil Castle, I'd been training with weaponry. I hadn't been aware anyone had told him.

Probably Thantrel or Sian. They were friends, and, though they'd not admit it, gossips. Or at least Thantrel Riis was.

"Speaking of flying—Lady Idun tore my wing. Ardal cleaned it and applied healing balms, but the wing won't support me."

His face hardened. "I'll carry you. The winds are up, so grab a fur cloak and whatever else you need, and let's go."

The items I wouldn't part with were few and thankfully still resting in my cloak pockets from my first failed escape attempt. Qildor averted his gaze, and it took no time at all to change into attire I wouldn't freeze in— woolen pants and layered woolen tunics. Once my boots were on, I secured my plain wool cloak around my shoulders and then added another fur-lined one. "I'm ready."

He held out his arm. Though my nerves lit up at the gesture, I forced my face to remain unchanged as I went to him and pressed my back against his chest, swallowing the pain that shot through my wing as I did so. He lifted me with ease as he walked to the window. Qildor took great care as he maneuvered our bodies through the broken glass and once he was sure we wouldn't get cut, his wings opened, and he flew.

Indeed, the winds were wicked, and the cold had deepened since that morning. It was so cold that my cheeks stung. I wondered how long we'd ride before we stopped.

Qildor landed us in the shadow of my tower where two horses, both midnight black, waited.

"How did you get another horse?" I asked as he gestured to the smaller mare.

"I stole her. Another reason we must hurry."

My lips parted. Qildor was a knight of the realm, and more than that, he was a standup gentlefae. For him to have stolen anything was unthinkable.

Apparently not, though. I mounted the mare and Qildor spurred his horse on toward the gate.

"Stay behind me," he said approvingly, because though we'd only gone about twenty steps, I'd already fallen in line. "If you hear anything, speak up." The wind dimmed his words, which would make hearing anyone approach difficult. "And keep those daggers—"

"Hey! What's this?!" a high-pitched male voice shouted.

"That's the jarl's wife!" another answered. "She's running again!"

"Bleeding skies." Qildor leapt, his wings teasing out of the protective cloak as he soared toward the guards.

One dove out of the way. The other raised his sword, the fool. He was outmatched. I did not have time to watch the fight, however, because the more cowardly guard scrambled to his feet, and upon seeing that his colleague was facing Qildor, rushed at me.

"No way we're getting yelled at for you!"

I pulled one of my daggers and hurled it at the guard. The blade hit its mark, right in his thigh, and the guard fell with a cry.

Knowing that his screaming would draw more people, I leapt from the mare and ran to the young male, kicking the blade he'd been carrying but had dropped out of his reach before I pressed my boot to his neck. He ceased screaming and stared up at me, jaw tight, body rigid.

"Don't scream, don't speak, don't even *whisper*, or I'll crush your windpipe," I threatened, hoping I would not have to do so.

Sayyida Virtoris had taught me about pressure points to knock out a fae. I'd much prefer to go that route, but to do so, I'd have to kneel, and despite the blade in his leg, he could attack me.

So instead, I kept my foot on the guard's neck and twisted in time to watch Qildor spin and dip and slice at the tendon at his opponent's ankle. The fae fell with a yelp, and Qildor was upon him, wrapping an arm around his neck. One of the pressure points was there.

The guard's eyelids fluttered, and my stomach tightened at how easily Qildor had taken down another soldier. How easily he protected himself and me.

"Those lessons paid off." Qildor set his opponent on the snow and approached me with such bare approval and pride on his face that my insides twisted in pleasure. "Hold your other dagger at his belly."

I did as the knight said, and when Qildor reached us, he motioned for me to remove my foot. The guard didn't so much as make a squeak as Qildor knelt behind him and pulled the faerie up enough to wrap his arm around the guard's neck. The second guard passed out more quickly than the first.

"We have maybe ten minutes before they wake." Qildor set the guard in the snow. "Their injuries will buy us more time, but we shouldn't squander it."

"Once we're off the grounds, we run." I leapt back on my horse.

Again, I stayed behind him as we led the horses to the gate. Though we were both alert and waiting for another altercation, no such thing occurred. We slipped through the gates and didn't bother shutting them behind us.

On the roads of Liekos, we urged the horses to go faster. Though I wasn't free yet, I grinned. It might be freezing, the wind biting, and I might have days ahead where I was uncomfortable or in danger, but I was out of the castle, away from my monster of a mother-in-law.

We slowed not too far from the gate and pulled up our hoods. So far, no alarms sounded, and once we were free of the city gates, we could gallop.

"Let me do the talking," Qildor said. "Keep your face hidden and slouch as you ride. Act like a commonborn."

I did as he said, and we approached the gates. To my surprise, no one called out. In fact, I didn't hear anyone in the area. And suddenly, I saw the guards, passed out atop the gate, one with his arm hanging over the edge.

"What in all the nine kingdoms?" I whispered just as the gate creaked open, and Qildor let out a chuckle.

"I see you wanted to help too," he said softly.

"She freed us," Ardal said, her head now poking through the slightest opening in the city gate. "The least we could do was spike the drink of those watching the city gates. The potion will last for hours and they'll be out the entire time, but you should still hurry."

My heart swelled. "Ardal, thank you."

She waved us through the gate, where, to my shock, twelve other goblins waited on the other side. They rode three to a pony, which was still too large for their small frames.

I blinked down at them. "What's going on?"

Ardal gave a sad smile. "Many of us already left, and some are still waiting to escape, but those here have no place to go, so we thought we might travel with you, Lady Marit?"

"You—you'd want to?"

"Your knight mentioned that a war was coming. That he thought change could come too. We have no tribe left, or none we'd go back to, and none of us can stand for what has happened to the goblins under the king's reign. Perhaps we can be a part of the change for our kind?"

War. Against my friends.

"If you insist," Qildor said. "We're traveling to the castle of House Balik. They're heavily fortified and a great distance from the capital."

I caught Ardal's eyes. "If you wish to join us, all the better."

CHAPTER 10

In the distance, washed in the muted colors of the sunset, an inn waited. Rundown and small though it appeared, I'd never been so happy to see shelter.

Our group of merry runaways had traveled through what remained of the previous night and all day long. No one wished to do more than stop for water or to relieve ourselves. Not when Lady Idun may very well have sent soldiers after us.

But now Liekos was far behind, and I couldn't travel another hour and not collapse in my saddle. The goblins looked just as tired. Actually, among us, only Qildor remained alert. I supposed many turns of knighthood gave him unmatched stamina.

"Where are we?" I asked the knight.

He shrugged a shoulder. "There are many small

villages like this one on the King's Road going south, and they all look much the same to me."

The goblins didn't seem to know either, and I gave up on finding out. The name of the village didn't matter much. All I wanted was a warm room and a bed.

"You may have to do some haggling to get us room in the stables," Ardal said, shattering my peaceful thoughts of warmth and a mattress.

I cringed, hating the idea of Ardal and the other goblins having to sleep outside on such a cold night, but knowing she was likely right.

On the whole, goblins were not permitted in most fae establishments and lived a life of nomadic freedom in the wilds of the kingdom. Leprechauns were the only exception.

"I'll make sure you have a place," I assured her.

We reached the inn, and the stablehand, a satyr youngling, rushed out. His horns were just starting to grow, putting him at about eight or nine turns old. The smile vanished from his face the moment he took in the goblins behind us.

"We need rooms," I rushed to speak first and put so much noble command in my tone that he blinked and turned back to me.

"I think there are some left," the youngling said. "But only for you and the knight. Goblins can't stay here."

"We have gold," I retorted, not about to take no for an answer. Especially not from a youngling who likely had little say in the matter.

His gaze darted to the inn before returning to me. He chewed on his lower lip. "You can ask the innkeeper, but I don't think it will matter."

I dismounted. "I'll be right back. Take care of the horses and ponies."

The youngling looked ready to say something else, but I gave him a glare I'd often used on my little brothers and the child set to his task.

"Do you require help?" Qildor asked.

"Not for this." My tone was confident.

If we failed to find rooms in the inn or the stables for the goblins, I'd not admit defeat. There had to be a home around here desperate enough for gold that they'd take in a few goblins for the night. It was a matter of finding one, though of course, the inn would be the most convenient.

Few fae roamed the downstairs tavern portion of the inn, though all of them turned to look my way as I entered. Despite having thrown on plain clothing before running away, I still bore the bearing of a lady, and that always garnered attention. I took it in stride and approached the bar, where an older male faerie waited.

"I'm looking for rooms for the night," I said.

"One left in the inn," he replied, his voice rumbly.

Only one? How? It wasn't busy in here at all!

"Three rooms caught fire," the faerie replied, clearly

anticipating my question. "The ones around back. We're not renting them yet."

"I see." Not ideal, but something I could work with. If they had a fire, they'd want gold to fix the place up. "Might I ask, how large?"

"Small. Just one bed."

"Right." I swallowed. I'd only ever shared a bed with my brothers, and then my husband. The latter experience had been traumatizing, and while I didn't think Qildor was capable of such actions, it still made me uncomfortable to share a bed with him.

Work it out later, I reminded myself.

"We'll take it," I said. "Though do you have room in your stables? And extra blankets? The others in my party wouldn't need much space."

The barkeeper's eyebrows arched. "How many are there?"

"Thirteen."

"That's a lot."

Best to come out with it. I didn't want this barkeeper to later discover goblins were in the stables and kick us out in the dead of night.

"Yes, well, they're goblins, you see. So they don't take up much room."

He snorted. "No space in the stables."

My blood warmed, and I gripped the side of the bartop. How predictable. And *infuriating.*

Ardal had become my friend, or at least friendly, and the goblins had helped save me. I wished better for them and felt ashamed that I'd never considered their race much before, but now wasn't the time to worry about changing the world. I only needed to change one mind about one thing. And I knew just the way to go about achieving my goal.

I reached into my cloak pocket, where half of the golden bracelets waited. The goblins hadn't wanted to carry them, which I didn't blame them for, but the pieces were too valuable to toss away, so I kept half and Qildor pocketed the others.

"Would these change your mind?" I put two golden bracelets on the table. "*Pure gold.*"

His eyes bulged, telling me all that I needed to know. "You're certain?"

"I am." Though the goblins had been slaves, they'd been Lady Triam's slaves, and that sort of female wouldn't have accepted anything less to show her possession over other beings. "If you don't believe me, ask that dwarf by the fire."

The barkeeper let out a hum, but didn't call the dwarf over. "Fine. They can stay in the stables and you in the room. But you have to be out at first light."

Fine by me. The further we are from Liekos, the better.

"I need food for them too," I said and didn't offer to pay more. The bracelets alone were valuable enough to repair the damaged rooms. He could throw in a few dinners.

He knew it too, for he didn't argue, just gestured to

the kitchen door at the left side of the short bar. "Stew and rolls is what we got."

I turned for the door, calling over my shoulder as I went. "I expect the bowls to be delivered to the stables. I'm going to go give them the news so that they may rest."

CHAPTER 11

We sat side by side at a table in front of the fire. With every crack and pop of the logs, my guilt mounted.

"I hate thinking of them out there," I said to Qildor, the only one in our party allowed inside the inn with me.

"I do too," he admitted. "But they're fed, sheltered, and you made sure they had mountains of blankets. They'll survive." He met my eyes. "And most important of all, they're free and safe."

True. But Fates, I still felt guilty.

"Do you think the Baliks will let them into Myrr?"

"Yes," Qildor said. "Once we tell them how the goblins helped you, which we will. You can be sure of that."

I took a bite of my stew. I was on my second helping and feeling warm and full. Soon, I'd only want for the bed upstairs. The single bed I had not mentioned yet to Qildor.

May as well get that over with.

"When I spoke to the barkeep, he said there was only one bed upstairs." I spoke into my bowl.

"Oh." Silence passed between us for a few heartbeats. "I'll sleep down here then."

I lifted my gaze. No doubt the barkeep would allow that with what we'd paid, but I couldn't allow Qildor to sleep on one of these uncomfortable wooden benches.

"No, it's fine," I assured him, despite my stomach tying up in knots. "We'll share. I'd feel safer with you in the room."

Safer, but still awkward.

The knight met my stare. "I don't like to think about what you've been through these last weeks, Marit. No one should have to endure what you have. So to make you feel safe, I'll stay in the room with you, but I'll be sleeping on the floor."

I swallowed, but saw that, in this, Qildor would be unmovable. Courtly. Stars, though Qildor was commonborn, he was a thousand times the gentlefae that my husband was. And as much as I didn't want him to be uncomfortable on the cold floor, I nodded my acceptance.

"I'll see if the barkeep has a bedroll. And more blankets, of course."

"That will do." He took a swig of his sour ale. "You

know, your brother and I once slept in a cave for a week."

My mouth dropped open. "You and Connan?"

He grinned slyly.

"You did not!" Rune would absolutely do that. But Connan? My brother was, to put it mildly, pampered. More so than me!

"I made him do it. Said it would strengthen him, and Connan might be prissy, but he liked that idea."

I smirked. Qildor was older than me by a turn, and older than Connan by two. My brother had always looked up to Qildor as an intriguing and influential older brother figure, so I suspected it didn't take too much to convince Connan if Qildor was the one doing the convincing.

"How though?" My parents would have never allowed such things. Not without guards accompanying their heir and his friend.

"We'd sneak out at night and sleep in the caves closest to the city. Then we'd get up at first light and run back. The gate guards saw us but never said anything. We amused them. Or maybe they thought their next lord needed some toughening up." Qildor grinned mischievously as he set down his bowl, his stew gone. "Sleeping on the floor upstairs will be nothing compared to that."

I laughed. "I won't waste another second feeling bad about it then."

He shouldered me, and the heat of his body rippled

through me, sending a shiver down my spine. "Don't. I'm a knight, Marit. I've endured worse."

Endured. My house words were '*the pack endures*', and they had never resonated more than in that moment. We were all enduring in some way. If war came, things would only get worse.

Not if. When.

"Thank you."

"For offering to sleep on the floor?"

"For *showing up*. I don't know how much longer I would have lasted in that place."

He took my hand, and I couldn't help but lean closer to him. To safety. To mutual respect. To someone who reminded me so much of home.

"You would have. You may not be a soldier, but you're strong." The surrounding air warmed in a way that wasn't from the flickering flames. I leaned closer. So did he, and I swore his eyes dipped to my lips.

We looked away as a loud crack of the log broke the spell between us. One I couldn't believe had begun to spin. I was still married and had been through so much at Jarl Triam's hands. To feel a romantic pull—no matter how slight—towards another at this time . . . It shouldn't be possible.

But then this was *Qildor*. Kind, caring, and stalwart, Qildor. A male who'd spent many nights at my family's table. A fae who had devoted his life to defending others.

There had once been something between the knight

and I. Perhaps there still was. Now wasn't the time to explore it, though. Not when I hadn't healed. Not when we had so far to go until we were safe. Not when the kingdom was on the brink of war.

He cleared his throat, as if he were trying to clear away the tension of the moment, and lifted his horn. "Another ale?"

I swallowed. "No, I'll go make sure a bedroll and blankets are delivered to our room. You can meet me up there when you're ready."

"Good idea."

I left him at the table, made my requests to the barkeep, and went to the stairs. The tavern had cleared out, leaving only the barkeep, Qildor, and a dwarf. I climbed the stairs, heart beating hard at what had almost happened between my first love and me.

THE NINE KINGDOMS OF ISILA

The Blood Kingdom - vampire
The Elven Kingdom - elves
The Winter Kingdom - fae of various races
The Autumn Kingdom - fae of various races
The Spring Kingdom - fae of various races
The Summer Kingdom - fae of various races
The Wolvea Kingdom - wolvea shifters
The Dragon Kingdom - dragon shifters

*** Each kingdom is colloquially described as a court, though technically, the court is a specific place or places in the larger kingdom.

Some kingdoms have additional names, such as the Winter Kingdom being called Winter's Realm or the Dragon Kingdom being called the Kingdom of Flame.

THE HIGH NOBILITY OF THE KINGDOM OF WINTER

HOUSE AABERG - ROYAL HOUSE
King Magnus Aaberg
Queen Inga Aaberg née Vagle

Children
Prince Rhistel Aaberg
Prince Vale Aaberg
Princess Saga Aaberg

The royal house is not a part of the Sacred Eight.[1] They do rely heavily on the families of the Sacred Eight but the royal house is distinct from all others.

Before the White Bear's Rebellion, House Aaberg was a member of the Sacred Eight. Since the rebellion House Riis took their place as a reward for loyalty to House Aaberg.

The Sacred Eight Families of Winter's Realm

*** Lord Sten Armenil - Warden of the North - Head of House**
*** Lady Orla Armenil née Balik**
Children
* Marit Armenil - female
* Connan Armenil - male
* Rune Armenil - male
* Tiril Armenil - female
* Jorunn Armenil - female
* Raemar Armenil - male

*** Lady Vaeri Ithamai - Warden of the East - Head of House**
*** Lord Tiarsus Itamai née Skau - deceased**
Children
* Hadia Ithamai - female
* Adila Ithamai - female

*** Lord Tadgh Balik - Warden of the South - Head of House**
*** Lady Kilyn Balik née Armenil**
Children
* Sian Balik - male
* Baenna Balik - female
* Eireann Balik - female

* Saoirse Balik - female
* Fionn Balik - male
* Garbhan Balik - male - deceased
* Carai Balik - female
* Filip Balik - squire to Prince Vale of House Aaberg - male
* Colm Balik - male

*** Lord Roar Lisika - Warden of the West - Head of House**
Unmarried
No children

*** Lord Leyv Riis - Head of House**
Unmarried
Children (only the children at court are included)
* Luccan Riis - male
* Arie Riis - male
* Thantrel Riis - non-binary

*** Lord Airen Vagle - Lord of Coin - Head of House**
*** Lady Eliana Vagle - deceased**
Children
* Queen Inga - married to King Magnus Aaberg
* Captain of the Royal Guard Eirwen Vagle - Father to Lady Calpurnia Vagle - his wife has passed to the afterworld
* Fival Vagle - acting lord in their family seat in the

midlands - male
* Selah Vagle - married to a wealthy Jarl in the
midlands - female

*** Lady Nalaea Qiren - Lady of Silks - Head of
House
* Lord Virion Qiren née Ithamai - deceased
Children**
* Aenesa Qiren - female
* Thalia Qiren - female
* Iro Qiren - female

*** Lady Fayeth Virtoris - Lady of Ships - Head of
House
* Lord Kailu Virtoris née Oridan, from the
Summer Court
Children**
* Vidar Virtoris - betrothed to Princess Saga of House
Aaberg - male
* Sayyida Virtoris - female
* Njal Virtoris - male
* Amine Virtoris - female

**EXTINCT GREATER HOUSES – ALL MEMBERS OF THESE
NOBLE HOUSES WERE KILLED DURING THE WHITE BEAR'S
REBELLION**

House Falk

King Harald's royal house

House Skau

Queen Revna's birth house. She married into House Falk and had six children with King Harald.

Beneath the Sacred Eight there are hundreds of lesser houses. These are led by jarls of various territories.

---

1. Prior to the White Bear's Rebellion, the Sacred Eight were actually the Sacred Nine, with House Skau being the ninth member, and House Falk being the royal house.

<u>The Winter Court (Crowns of Magic Universe)</u>

A Kingdom of Frost and Malice

A Lord of Snow and Greed

A Hallow of Storm and Ruin

A Tower of Gold and Goblins - companion novella

A Crown of Ice and Fury

Book 5, TBA

<u>Coven of Shadows and Secrets (Crowns of Magic Universe)</u>

Seeker of Secrets

Hunted by Darkness

History of Witches

Marked by Fate

Kingdoms of Sin

Bound by Destiny

<u>Standalone Novels</u>

Curse of the Fae Prince (The Spring Court: Crowns of Magic Universe)

<u>Spellcasters Spy Academy Series (Magic of Arcana Universe)</u>

A Legacy Witch: Year One

A Marked Witch: Internship

A Rebel Witch: Year Two

A Crucible Witch: Year Three

The Spellcasters Spy Academy Boxset

<u>The Wonderland Court Series (Magic of Arcana Universe)</u>

Alice the Dagger

Alice the Torch

<u>The Bonegate Series - A Fanged Fae sister series</u>

Hawk Witch

Assassin Witch

Traitor Witch

Illuminator Witch

The Bonegates Series Boxset

<u>The Royal Quest Series</u>

Dragon Prince

Dragon Magic

Dragon Mate

Dragon Betrayal

Dragon Crown

Dragon War

About the Author

Ashley lives in the lush and green Pacific Northwest with her husband, their dog, and the house ghost that sometimes makes appearances in her charming, old home.

When she's not writing fantasy novels she enjoys traveling the world, reading, kicking butt at board games, and frequenting taquerias.

For all the latest releases and updates, subscribe to Ashley's newsletter, The Coven. You can also find her Facebook group, Ashley's Reader Coven.

www.ingramcontent.com/pod-product-compliance
Lightning Source LLC
Chambersburg PA
CBHW031546310726
48971CB00008B/2645